First Strike

The Erotic Prequel to *Striking Distance*

By Pamela Clare

FIRST STRIKE

The Erotic Prequel to *Striking Distance*

Published by Pamela Clare, 2014

Cover image by Jenn LeBlanc of Studio Smexy™
Cover design by Seductive Designs

ISBN-10: 0990377105
ISBN-13: 9780990377108

This book is dedicated to the female orgasm.

The world would be a more just and beautiful place if women everywhere were free to enjoy their own sensuality and choose their sexual destinies, protected from the scourges of child marriage, sexual violence, and genital mutilation.

AUTHOR'S NOTE

Let me warn you right now—*First Strike* ends with a cliffhanger. It's the erotic prequel for *Striking Distance* (I-Team #6), which will be available on Nov. 5, 2013—hopefully not too long of a wait. Here's the story of how this came to be.

Striking Distance was one of the most challenging books I've ever written. By the time I was done, I had easily two pages of discarded text for every page I submitted to my editor. Sometimes that's how it goes.

Among those discarded pages was the first prologue I'd written. It introduced readers to Laura Nilsson, a broadcast journalist, and Javier Corbray, an active-duty Navy SEAL, and told the story of how they met. When I was many pages into that prologue, I realized I had a big problem. For starters, it was much too long. Also, I would have to have two prologues for the story to start where I wanted it to start. Together, the two prologues would span a period of four years. No novel should start with twenty pages of prologue. So, I reluctantly cut the initial prologue, only referring to the events as backstory in *Striking Distance*.

Sometimes writers have to make tough choices.

After finishing *Striking Distance* in June 2013, I went back through the material I had cut from the story, looking for fun "extras" to post on my blog, and I rediscovered how very much I had liked the story's first, original prologue. I decided to take those pages and transform them into a prequel, telling not just the highlights of the weekend when Laura and Javier meet, but the whole story. I knew that diehard I-Team readers would want to know about the magical weekend that binds Laura and Javier together, and I thought it would give me a chance to do something I hadn't done before—ratchet up the sensuality and write an erotic short story.

And that's what you're about to read—an erotic novella about the weekend Laura and Javier meet. I've taken the original prologue and expanded it, turning up the heat and allowing myself to play with language that doesn't usually make it into my books. I hope you'll enjoy the result.

As I mentioned, Dear Reader, this story ends with a cliffhanger. You won't find a "happily ever after" here. I know people sometimes find cliffhangers irritating. Yes, I have seen those "I hate cliffhanger" Facebook memes. But, given the fact that this is a prequel, there really wasn't any way around that.

Fortunately, *First Strike* is being released a couple of weeks prior to *Striking Distance*, so the wait won't be long. Also, given that the final prologue to *Striking Distance* is available on my website at this very moment, you will be able to alleviate the cliffhanger stress by simply going to my website and reading what happens next.

Also, you can choose to read this after *Striking Distance*, in which case it will likely feel especially poignant to you. Yes, I know, that's like asking a woman to save that piece of chocolate for later when she wants to eat it *now*. It's just an idea.

Okay, fine. Forget I said that.

Regardless of when you read *First Strike*—before or after *Striking Distance*—I hope you enjoy the story of these two people who meet and enjoy a wild weekend of "no strings" sex that becomes the foundation for redemption and enduring love.

Happy reading!

Pamela Clare

September 17, 2013

CHAPTER ONE

Dubai City, Dubai
United Arab Emirates
July 14, 2009

Javier Corbray walked into the ICON Bar in the Radisson Blu Hotel, his gaze traveling over the dim interior, taking it all in at once—the upscale décor, the busy wait staff, the near-to-capacity crowd of expats enjoying Happy Hour. It wasn't his scene. He wasn't even sure what he was doing in Dubai. He'd be back in the States now if he hadn't let JG talk him into playing tourist.

"You've *got* to see Dubai City," JG had said. "The buildings, the expat nightlife, the luxury cars—that place will blow your mind. Did I mention the indoor ski resort?"

Only about five times.

The city *was* amazing. Burj Al Arab. The Jumeirah Emirates Towers hotel. Al Kazim Towers. The artificial island of Palm Jumeirah with its long central avenue. Burj Khalifa, soon to be the world's tallest building.

The city dripped with wealth—oil dollars and foreign investment. But Javier would rather be putting together a barbecue with his dad in his folks' backyard in the South Bronx or home in San Diego than wandering around Dubai City in the 105-degree heat staring at architecture. And when it came to the beaches, nothing here could compare to the beaches of Puerto Rico.

Still, being a tourist for a few days wasn't a bad idea. He could use a little decompression time. It had been a long and rough deployment, one that had seen him and the other men of Delta Platoon caught between the mandate to win hearts and minds and their primary mission as SEALs—to kick ass and take names.

At least they hadn't lost anyone this time around.

A young man approached him, menu in hand. "Just one tonight?"

Javier nodded.

"This way, please." The man led him to a vacant table for two in the back of the restaurant not far from the emergency exit.

Javier sat with his back to the wall. It was instinctive for him—taking a defensive position, staying aware of his surroundings. He was no more conscious of doing it than he was of breathing.

He wanted a burger and a Heineken, but finding neither on the menu, he ordered steamed clams, a New York strip, and a pint of Vicaris Tripel instead.

A Filipino server quickly brought his beverage, the sight of the amber liquid and creamy, white head almost making Javier moan. He hadn't had a beer since before Delta Platoon had deployed last November. He raised the pint glass to his mouth and drank, foam tickling his upper lip, beer sliding, smooth and cold, down his throat.

Oh, hell, yeah.

He lowered the glass, licked the foam off his upper lip, a longing he'd had for months finally satisfied. He looked up—and recognized her the moment he saw her.

Laura Nilsson.

The Baghdad Babe.

That's what U.S. troops called her. They'd given her the nickname back in 2007 during The Surge, when she'd arrived in Baghdad and begun nightly live broadcasts from outside the Green Zone. Tall and slender with pale blond hair, big ice-blue eyes, a sweet face, and even sweeter curves, she had probably served as the fantasy for a thousand combat jacks, though not Javier's. He preferred dark-haired women with a bit more meat on their bones, women who had something to shake when they danced *bomba*.

What Javier *did* admire about Ms. Nilsson was her reporting. She was absolutely fearless, traveling to places most journalists refused to go, tackling stories that other reporters wouldn't touch or didn't see, giving the people back home the big picture on this war, telling it like it was. It helped that she had a security team and knew a half-dozen languages, including Arabic, Farsi, German, and French.

Javier sipped his beer, watching as the host escorted her to a table marked "Reserved" just a few tables away from where he sat. She wore a sleeveless black dress that hinted at the curves beneath and showed off her toned arms and slender legs. Her long blond hair hung down her back, its gentle waves held in place by a barrette, a leather handbag over her shoulder, sandals revealing polished pink toenails.

Did you just look her up and down, cabrón?

Yeah, he had.

He couldn't blame himself. Back-to-back deployments made it tough to have any kind of sex life. It had been more than a year since he'd gotten laid—something he was suddenly very conscious of.

Ms. Nilsson's gaze passed over the room, connecting with his. And for one startling moment, he found himself looking into a pair of cool, blue eyes. He felt his body tense ever so slightly, the intelligence behind those eyes seeming to assess him before she looked away.

She sat and smiled up at the server, the same Filipino kid who'd brought Javier his beer. "Just the usual, Bayani. Thank you."

If Javier hadn't recognized her face, he certainly would have recognized her voice—soft and feminine, but with that undercurrent of steel that made millions of viewers take her every word seriously.

She drew one of those fancy iPhones out of her handbag, turned it on, and began to poke intermittently at the screen, probably checking her email. She glanced up and smiled at the server when he returned with a glass of white wine. "Thank you."

Aware he was staring, Javier dug into his steamed clams the moment they arrived at his table, buttery goodness exploding in his mouth with every bite. He could live without the opulence and the fancy architecture that were such a part of Dubai City. But the food and brew?

Oh, yeah. He could get used to this.

He finished the clams just as his steak arrived. He ordered another beer, his gaze working its way back to Ms. Nilsson, who was eating a salad and sipping her wine. She was reading something on her smartphone, her attention focused. He willed himself to look away, turning his attention to the laughing crowd of Westerners, British accents mingling with Australian, Italian, and what sounded like German.

Then Javier saw something he didn't like.

He wasn't the only man in the restaurant watching her.

Laura Nilsson took another sip of her wine, relieved to see her investigation was coming together. It had taken months to make contact with the village elders, to earn their trust. At first, they had all refused to talk to her, fearing reprisals from the Taliban. But eventually one outraged father had come forward and told a heartbreaking story of how Taliban leaders had forced him at gunpoint to hand over two of his daughters. The girls, eight and ten years old, had been forced into marriage to two different men, raped over the course of a week, and then divorced and left behind. When the villagers had gone to the Afghan government for redress, the Taliban leaders had claimed that the farmer owed them money. Giving away daughters in payment of debts was a long-established tradition in Afghanistan, and so the government had done nothing.

Laura knew this was far from the first time such a thing had happened. Taliban fighters were using small villages as harems, abusing marriage and divorce laws for the sake of sex, preying on defenseless girls as young as eight and nine.

It made her sick.

She tapped out a quick email to Nico, the head of her security detail, asking for an update on her visa snarls and letting him know she had a date and time for her visit to the village. She would interview the girls and their father in hopes of exposing this abuse—and generating international pressure for the Afghan government to stop it.

A shadow fell across the table.

She glanced up, expecting to see Bayani with a pitcher to refill her water glass. Instead, she found herself looking up at two big men with heavy mustaches. Both appeared to be in their late forties or early fifties, their dark hair graying, their faces ruddy from sunburn and too much alcohol. One wore a blue short-sleeved shirt with black slacks and a black striped tie, the other a gray suit.

"You are Laura Nilsson." The one in the suit held out his hand, his accent distinctly Russian.

Why did people think that because they recognized someone, they had a right to intrude on that person's space?

Irritated but not wanting to be rude, Laura shook the man's beefy hand. She spoke some Russian, but opted for English, afraid that speaking their language would only encourage them. "I'm sorry, but I'm working and not—"

"Yuri," the other one said, interrupting her and extending his hand as well. "I always watch you in the TV when I am in America."

She stood, shook his hand, too. "It's nice to meet you both, but I'm afraid I don't have time to talk now. I'd like to be left alone to—"

"You are very brave woman." Yuri pointed to his companion. "Nikolai and I are petroleum engineers working on the big oil project here. We come from Russia."

No kidding.

Nikolai sat, an aggressive gesture. "Maybe you want to know more about our project, report on it for your news?"

They weren't taking the hint.

Laura looked for Bayani, saw that he was on the other side of the room. All she had to do was get his attention, and the men would be escorted out of the restaurant. If they caused a scene, they'd be arrested and deported.

She tried to keep things civil. "I'm sorry, but that's not the kind of news I cover. I would like to have a quiet dinner, so I'm asking you to leave."

"We join you, maybe buy you a drink?" Yuri started to pull out a chair.

A hand shot out of nowhere and held the chair in place.

"The lady asked you to leave."

It was *him*.

Laura had noticed him the moment she'd walked in and had taken more than one covert glance. He stood out in a room full of men in suits— and not just because he was so tall. He was dressed differently, too, wearing a pair of jeans and a T-shirt, the black cotton stretching over the muscles of his chest. His skin and eyes were brown, his dark hair cut short. He had high cheekbones, full lips, and a square jaw, the combination both masculine and exotic. She'd guessed he was from Latin America, perhaps Brazilian, but his accent told her he was from the States. Given his physique, she was pretty sure he was military—or an operative from a private security contractor.

Now he stood between her and Yuri, his expression hard.

Was he trying to *rescue* her?

She fought not to roll her eyes.

Men.

Not wanting this to escalate into chest-thumping and head-butting, she did her best to smooth over the situation. "They were just leaving."

Nikolai got to his feet, he and Yuri glaring at the man. "Who the fuck are you?"

"I'm the one who's going to kick your ass unless you do what the lady asks."

So they'd reached chest-thumping already.

Helvete! Damn!

Laura found herself holding her breath, hoping Nikolai and Yuri weren't so drunk and stupid as to start a brawl and get themselves or someone else hurt. They could all end up in jail on any number of charges—drinking alcohol, disturbing the peace, disrupting a place of business. An arrest would almost certainly lead to deportation, maybe even prison time. And that would have a devastating impact on Laura's career.

Dubai was a nation of contradictions and illusions where everything was permitted, but nothing was legal. You could order alcohol, but if you got into trouble, you'd end up in jail for drinking it. You could walk around wearing the same clothes you'd wear at home, but if someone complained that you were dressed immodestly, you might be deported. Women could work and move freely throughout the city, but if they were raped and reported it, they—not the rapist—would likely go to jail for it. The difference between enjoying a peaceful stay and being arrested and deported sometimes came down to a single interaction with police.

She flew through Dubai a half-dozen times a year, the emirate serving as a kind of staging area for trips to Iraq, Pakistan, and Afghanistan. If she were deported and barred from re-entering, it would be very hard to do her job. She'd fought like hell to get where she was today, and she wasn't going to let anything destroy what she'd accomplished—certainly not a couple of drunk Russians or some guy with a hero complex.

Laura watched Yuri's face turn red, saw Nikolai's nostrils flare.

Beside her, Mr. Chivalry hadn't budged, but there was a tension about him that told her he was more than ready to take both men down.

Nikolai tossed back the last of his drink, glanced over his shoulder, and seemed to remember where he was. He spoke to Yuri in Russian. "Come. We don't want to cause a scene. This bitch isn't worth it. We don't want to be deported."

Still visibly angry, the two men turned and walked away.

Laura let out a breath, then looked up at her rescuer, tension turning to irritation. "You didn't need to intervene. I didn't need your help. What if you had provoked a fight? You'd have ended up in a Dubai jail."

"I've been in worse places." He held out a hand. "Javier Corbray. And you're welcome, Ms. Nilsson."

So he had recognized her.

Laura looked into his eyes, awareness arcing between them as she took his hand and repeated his name. "Javier Corbray."

They stood there for a moment, he still holding her hand, she not drawing it away.

"I guess I'll let you get back to work." He gave her a nod, released her hand, and turned to walk back to his table.

Laura suddenly felt like a jerk. No, she hadn't needed him to save her, but he hadn't known that. He'd intervened believing he was truly helping her—and he'd apparently done so without expecting anything in return. If he'd been trying to hit on her, he wouldn't be halfway back to his table now.

"So that's it? You're just going to rescue me and go?"

CHAPTER TWO

Some part of Javier couldn't believe it. He was sitting in an upscale hotel restaurant in Dubai City having a conversation with Laura Nilsson.

He couldn't take his eyes off her. Those dimples in her cheeks when she smiled. The soft curve of her lips. The column of her throat. The play of light on her silky blond hair. Those perfect blue eyes. Hell, she even smelled good—clean, soft, sweet. He wanted to take her up to his room, lift that black dress over her head, and spend hours exploring every inch of her body.

How could he ever have thought her anything but beautiful?

Clearly he'd been an idiot.

"What made you decide to become a TV journalist?" Given the X-rated ideas chasing through his mind, he was surprised his brain was functioning enough for him to keep up with the conversation. But in truth, she was easy to talk to, not at all the Valkyrie he'd imagined she would be.

She smiled as she answered. "When I was thirteen, there was a fire in the building across the street. Swedish TV sent a reporter. I watched as she interviewed the families. Most of them had lost everything. She was moved to tears by a little boy who was sobbing about the kitten his parents hadn't been able to save. But when she went on the air, she was so calm and professional. She made everyone else in the country care about what had happened to those people. I decided that night I wanted to be like her, to share people's stories with the world and make them care."

Javier found himself hanging on her every word.

You want her.

Hell, yeah, he did. What man wouldn't?

Did she want him?

Why in the hell was he asking himself that question?

Dubai was not the place for a quick fling unless he wanted to risk flogging and a stint in jail, not to mention a demotion in rank when he got out. Creating an international incident by fucking around was not what his commander expected of him. Besides, a woman like Laura probably wanted some kind of commitment, and Javier wasn't interested in a relationship.

Sex? Yeah. Strings? Nah, man. It just wasn't for him.

He'd learned the hard way that SEALs and long-term relationships did not go together. "You grew up in Sweden?"

"I have dual citizenship." Her fingers traced a distracting line up and down the moist stem of her wine glass. "What about you? You haven't told me what you do."

He grinned. "No, I haven't."

And he wouldn't.

He took OPSEC—operational security—seriously. He never shared the fact that he was a special operator with people who didn't need to know, and he sure as hell wouldn't talk about it in public when his country was at war.

When he said nothing more, her sweet mouth went pouty. "All right then, keep your secrets."

Realizing what she might be thinking and not wanting to come across as some creep, he reached out and almost took her hand before he remembered where they were. The Naval Special Warfare travel advisory on Dubai warned service members to avoid so much as touching people of the opposite sex in public, apart from a simple handshake.

He rested his hand on the table close to hers. "I'm not dangerous."

One blond eyebrow arched.

Okay, so threatening those two Russians made what he'd just said seem like a lie.

He leaned closer. "I'm not a danger to *you*."

Her lips curved in a slow smile that made his blood ignite. "Oh, I don't believe that for a second."

What was it about men who gave off that "don't fuck with me" vibe that made Laura want to do just that?

"You didn't like Jumeirah Beach?" For a man who'd come to Dubai City to see the sights, he didn't seem very impressed.

"Nah, not really." He raised his beer mug and finished the glass, Laura's gaze drawn first to his flexing bicep, then to his moist lips. "Growing up, I spent summers at my grandmother's place in Humacao. You want to see a beach, come to Puerto Rico."

So he was Puerto Rican—probably a mix of Taíno Indian, African, and Spanish.

"I'm sure it's beautiful."

He nodded, smiled, looking into her eyes. "A lover's paradise."

A bolt of heat shot through her belly, her pulse skipping.

He made the words sound erotic, pronouncing every syllable slowly, the warmth in his eyes signaling that he wanted her as much as she wanted him.

Surprised by the intensity of her own physical reaction, she raised her glass to her lips, only to find it empty.

"Let me buy you another."

She set the glass down. "I'd like that. Thanks."

She watched as he made his way through the crowded restaurant toward the bar to get another glass of wine for her and another beer for himself, his perfect, muscular ass shifting beneath the denim of his jeans as he walked, his movements sleek, confident. People stepped aside for him, as if they knew instinctively that they shouldn't cross him.

But he wasn't arrogant. Most men who were ripped and sexy like Javier had egos to match, standing at the center of their own vain little worlds. But Javier hadn't shown a hint of swagger. Instead, he'd asked her a half-dozen questions about her job, seeming genuinely interested in her answers. He even knew about some of her bigger stories—her exposé on the Pentagon's failure to supply soldiers with body armor, her investigation into the group of servicemen who'd been running a protection racket in Baghdad. She sensed something deeper in Javier, something that went beyond his good looks and charm, something real.

God, he turned her on.

From the moment he'd sat at her table, her mind had begun spinning sexual fantasies of the two of them together. Everything about him seemed to draw her in—his smooth skin, his voice, the stubble on his square jaw, his clean scent, those full lips. What would they feel like when he kissed her, tasted her, went down on her?

The very thought made her wet.

She'd always been careful about the men she allowed into her bed, sometimes going months and even years between lovers. Her job put her in the public eye, and the last thing she wanted was to leave a trail of men who would watch the news, point to her, and say to their buddies, "Yeah, I slept with her. I fucked the Baghdad Babe."

Her career didn't leave a lot of time for men, anyway. She had dreams of one day being a news anchor or perhaps even hosting an evening news program. She had no desire to get married, settle down, and have kids, and that meant she needed to steer clear of men who might mistake her interest for something more than sexual.

She watched as he paid for the drinks and then started back toward the table, another glass of chardonnay in one hand, a mug of beer in the other.

Would he be good in bed?

Pondering that question made her ache inside.

Oh, yes, he would be.

She couldn't say what made her so sure of that. Maybe it was the way he paid attention to every word she said. Maybe it was the way he moved, so in control of his own body. Maybe it was the heat in his eyes when he looked at her. But she had a feeling that if she ended up in bed with him, he would make it well worth her while.

She crossed her legs, squeezed, trying to appease the ache, but that only made it worse, the feeling of arousal between her thighs impossible to ignore.

Pull it together, Nilsson.

Of course, there was no way for them to hook up—not here. Unmarried sex was illegal in Dubai. It was even illegal for unrelated men and women to be alone together. They couldn't just get into the elevator, head to her room, and get it on. If they were caught, they'd go to jail, maybe even be flogged.

And wouldn't that make for a nice news teaser?

Laura Nilsson arrested in Dubai for illicit sex with man she barely knew. Hormones to blame. Film at eleven.

She ran the words through her mind and found herself wondering again what Javier did for a living. Was he Delta Force? An Army Ranger? A Green Beret?

Most U.S. servicemen trusted her enough to tell her what they did for a living, but Javier wasn't one of them. That meant the work he did was highly classified—or that he worked for a private contractor that specialized in covert ops.

He could be an arms dealer for all you know.

There was no doubt. He *was* dangerous.

Somehow that thought left her feeling even more aroused.

You need to buy a battery-operated boyfriend.

Even if she'd had one, she wouldn't have been able to bring it along on her travels. She was pretty sure she'd get into less trouble if she were caught smuggling an AK-47 into Dubai than if she were found in possession of a vibrator.

Javier handed her the wine glass, his warm fingers grazing hers, striking sparks off her skin. He slid into the seat across from her. "This place gets crowded."

She glanced around them. "It's Friday night. Most of the city is shut down. Expats have to do something with themselves."

"Cheers." He raised his beer glass and drank.

Her gaze locked with his, desire for him driving all other thoughts from her mind.

She set her glass aside, leaned toward him, lowering her voice to a whisper, her pulse spiking as she shared what was on her mind. "Will this conversation get awkward if I tell you how very much I want to fuck you?"

J avier leaned against the paneled elevator wall, Laura's extra key card in his pocket next to the condoms he'd bought in the bar's restroom. Anticipation coiled inside him, made his blood run hot, his mind filling with erotic images. Laura naked on all fours, head down, ass up. Laura on her back, her thighs on his shoulders as he went down on her. Laura riding him, her breasts in his hands.

You're loco, *Corbray. If you get caught…*

He glanced covertly at the security camera, knowing that no one was actually watching to make sure he got off at the sixteenth floor instead of the nineteenth.

Room 1927.

She was waiting for him there.

And, God, he hoped she was naked.

No, he hoped she hadn't removed a thing. *He* wanted to undress her.

Hell, he didn't care. He just wanted to be there, in her room, inside *her*.

He paced the length of the elevator, the car not moving nearly fast enough.

Fifth floor. Sixth. Seventh.

¡Puñeta! Fuck!

When was the last time he'd hooked up with a woman he'd met in a bar?

He'd been twenty-three going on stupid. He'd met a pretty *chula*, taken her back to his place, and had a night of empty, meaningless sex that had been followed by a week of hoping he'd never see her again.

But Laura Nilsson wasn't just some college girl. She was an accomplished journalist, a household name back in the U.S. Hell, half the world knew who she was. Why had she chosen him tonight when she could have had any man in that restaurant? He was just a *Boricua* from the South Bronx. She had money, good looks, brains.

Worried you won't measure up, pendejo?

Fourteenth floor. Fifteenth. Sixteenth.

He didn't think he'd ever met a woman who was as direct as she was. First, she'd told him she wanted to fuck him. Then she'd laid down her conditions.

I want you to understand that I don't plan on getting married or having kids. This weekend—it's just a weekend. Nothing more. Okay?

No strings. That works for me, too.

Truth be told, it turned him on that she knew what she wanted.

Eighteenth. Nineteenth.

The elevator car stopped, a tiny bell giving a *ding* as the doors opened.

He stepped out to find the hallway empty, not a security camera in sight.

He glanced at the polished, bronze-plated sign on the wall and followed the directions down the long corridor toward her room, drawing the key card from his pocket and slipping it into the lock.

A buzz.

The light flashed green.

He opened the door and walked in.

She stood just inside the door, the bedside lamp lighting the luxurious room behind her, spilling over the neatly made bed. She was barefoot but still dressed, her pupils dilated, her lips parted, her breathing rapid and shallow. She took one step toward him, threw her arms around his neck and rose on tiptoe to kiss him.

He drew her hard against him, his lips meeting hers for a kiss that lit him on fire—skin, blood, and bones. Her lips were soft, her clever tongue teasing his, her body sweet in his arms. He felt her shift, one of her hands fumbling with his zipper.

The woman wasn't wasting time. Fine by him.

He wanted her *now*.

Without breaking the kiss, he slid a hand into his pocket, drew out a condom, and pressed it into the palm of the hand that had freed his cock. While she took care of that, he took care of her, backing her against the wall and reaching beneath her black dress to cup her through the irritating silk of her panties.

¡Diache! Holy shit!

She was already wet.

He grabbed the elastic band and broke it with a jerk, ripping her panties off her body and tossing them aside. Then he let his fingers explore the slick sweetness of her pussy, nudging apart her plump labia, teasing her swollen little clit, sliding a finger deep inside her.

She gasped, gave a hungry little whimper, spreading her legs for him, her hand rolling a condom down the aching length of his cock as he fingered her.

When the condom was in place, he grabbed her ass, lifted her off the floor, and pinned her against the wall with his weight, her legs wrapping tightly around his waist as she opened herself to him. And with a groan, he buried himself inside her.

She turned her head to the side, her cheek pressing into the wall, her voice a breathy whisper. *"Oh. God!"*

She felt so damned good, her pussy closing around his cock like a fist. Tight. Hot. Sweet.

He moved inside her, giving her time to get used to him—three slow thrusts that almost blew his mind. And then he was driving into her hard and fast, fucking her with an urgency that took him by surprise, aware only of her and his need for her.

The musky scent of her arousal. The sweet sound of her moans. The tightening of her thighs around his waist. The bite of her nails through the cloth of his shirt. The look of sexual bliss on her face.

Her exhales became a whispered plea. *"Fuck me! Fuck me! Fuck me!"*

Faster, harder he thrust into her, his hips a piston. He fought to hold on, fought to finish her first, willing himself to last long enough. His mouth found the sensitive skin beneath her ear, kissing, sucking, biting. She felt so good, tasted so good.

He felt her stiffen, heard her breath break, and had just enough time to silence her cry with a kiss. She arched in his arms, her inner muscles clenching around him as she came, driving him headlong toward the brink—and over the shimmering edge.

Orgasm slammed through him with all the force and heat of a blast wave. He buried his face in her throat, groaned against her skin, his body seeming to come apart in her arms. And for a time, they stayed that way— him inside her, his face pressed against her throat, her fingers in his hair.

He lifted his head and looked into a pair of beautiful blue eyes. And he could see she was as surprised as he by what had just happened.

"I'm not done with you." She kissed him.

Javier kissed her back. "I sure as hell hope not."

CHAPTER THREE

Laura felt him withdraw from her and lower her to her feet. She caught just a glimpse of his cock—still half-hard, wet, uncut—the sight of him making her pulse quicken. Then he turned and walked to the bathroom to clean up, condom in hand, her gaze following him.

Hadn't she known he'd be good in bed? They hadn't even reached the bed yet, and her body was still humming with satisfaction at what had been one of the most intense orgasms of her life.

At five-foot-ten, she wasn't exactly petite. No man had ever done what Javier had just done, lifting her off the ground and fucking her up against the wall like that. For that matter, no man had ever ripped her panties off her body, as if he couldn't wait long enough for her to take them off. What Javier had done had left her feeling intensely feminine, something inside her melting to find a man who could handle her sexually aggressive nature, even surpass it.

She got aroused again just thinking about it.

"Wow." His voice came back to her from the bathroom, and she knew he'd discovered the sunken tub. "My room doesn't have one of these."

As big as a twin-size bed and two feet deep, it had Greek columns that reached to the ceiling from each of its four corners, its tiles painted in ruby reds, sun yellows, emerald greens, and lapis blues.

The toilet flushed, and she heard water running in the sink.

Javier stepped out of the bathroom. "I had to flush it."

"What?"

"The condom." He walked toward her, the top button of his jeans still undone, a trail of hair disappearing behind his waistband. "I didn't want to toss it in the trash where the maid could find it."

"Oh. Yes. Good idea." She hadn't thought of that. She supposed now was a good time to bring this up. "I use long-term contraception, so I'm protected. As long as you know you're safe, we don't need to use condoms."

He reached for her. "Believe it or not, I don't make a habit of this. I've been tested, so I know I'm clean. Now where were we?"

"I was about to undress you." She reached for him.

He caught her wrists, stopped her. "No, I was about to undress *you*."

She was used to being in control, used to taking the lead, but something about him—his absolute confidence, his physical size and strength—made her want to yield.

She had just a moment to register that surprising fact before he kissed her, his lips caressing hers softly this time, his hands catching the cloth of her dress. He broke the kiss, stepped back, drew her dress over her head, letting it fall to the floor, leaving her to stand there wearing only her black silk bra.

His gaze slid slowly down her body, fixing on her pubic area and the trimmed triangle of dark blond curls there, before sliding back up her body again. "Turn around."

She did as he asked, moving slowly, watching his face over her shoulder, his hungry expression leaving no doubt that he liked what he saw.

He reached out, unclasped her bra.

She caught it, held it in place over her breasts just to tease him.

But he seemed to have enough to keep him busy, one big hand cupping her bare ass while the other reached round, splayed across her belly, and drew her backward.

She leaned back against him, felt the heat of his lips against the skin of her shoulder, the hand that had cupped her ass sliding over her hip and down to her pussy. His fingers began to play with her in slow strokes, making the most of the wetness her orgasm had left behind. Her clit was extra sensitive as it always was after she came. He seemed to know this, his teasing delicate but relentless.

And her arousal began to build again.

She moaned, her head falling back on his strong shoulder, his tongue hot and slick as he nipped and licked the skin beneath her ear.

"I want to feel you. Drop the bra, *bella*."

Bella.

Spanish for "beautiful."

She did as he demanded, black silk falling forgotten to her feet.

He slid his free hand up the skin of her rib cage, groaning when he found her breast, squeezing it gently, his touch making her nipples draw tight.

She had no idea how long they stood there like that, her head resting against his shoulder, one of his hands busy between her thighs, the other playing with her breasts. Her hips began to move, her body greedy for release. "Oh, God, don't tease me."

He chuckled. "Think I can keep you on the brink like this all night, *bella*?"

Her head rolled back and forth against his shoulder in protest. "No! No, no."

"Then let me taste you."

Whispered against her ear, the words almost made her knees go weak. "*Yes.*"

He scooped her into his arms as if she were weightless, reaching the bed in two strides. Then he dropped her on the mattress, grabbed her ankles, and dragged her toward him till her ass was even with the edge of the bed. He drew her legs apart, forced her knees to bend, his gaze fixed on her exposed and aching pussy, the expression on his face making her heart thud. "*Jesus!*"

Anticipation coiled tightly in her belly as he dropped to his knees, guided her feet so they rested on his shoulders, and parted her with his fingers

He gave her a long, slow lick. "Mmm."

Her insides clenched.

She reached down and slid her fingers into his dark hair, her eyes drifting shut as he explored her with lips and tongue.

Oh, but the man knew how to use his mouth! The velvet friction of his tongue against the opening of her vagina. The sweet tug of his lips on her clit. The gentle suckling. One sensation collided with the next, her breath coming in pants and moans, her hips lifting off the bed, her body shaking.

It had been so long since she'd felt like this—sexually strung-out, her body hovering in that bright shimmering place that came just before an orgasm. The pleasure was almost unbearable, every stroke of his lips over her clit making her moan, her vagina aching to be stretched, penetrated, filled. "Fuck me with your fingers!"

He gave a groan, two thick fingers sliding inside her and moving in time to the action of his mouth, driving into her deep and hard.

Oh, God, yes!

She came with a cry, climax surging through her in rippling golden waves, her inner muscles gripping his fingers, his mouth keeping up its rhythm until she was breathless and spent. She lay there for a moment, floating.

She heard the sound of a zipper and opened her eyes to find him standing over her, his body naked at last, his gaze fixed on her face. Her vagina clenched—hard. She took in the sight of him from the muscles of his nearly hairless chest to his six-pack to his erect cock, its engorged head exposed and straining. And it didn't matter that she'd already come twice—and come hard.

She wanted him again.

She was about to get onto her hands and knees and take him into her mouth. But he caught her legs with the crooks of his arms, pushing her knees back as his body came down on hers, his cock sliding into her until that engorged tip pressed against her cervix, his balls resting against her ass.

She tensed, afraid he would go so deep that it would hurt. But then he rocked forward, pushing her knees back to her shoulders until her bottom was lifted off the bed, the shift in position angling her hips to make more room for him inside her. And he held her there, strong arms pressed against the bed, his gaze locked with hers.

"Ooh!" It was all she could say, her nails digging into his biceps.

"*¡Ay Dios mio!* You feel *so* … damned … good." His voice was strained, his muscles tense.

And then he was moving, slowly at first, his momentum building until he was pounding himself into her, burying his cock to the hilt again and again, stroking every inch of her vagina, the friction carrying her headlong into another climax.

A half smile curved his lips as she came, his male satisfaction at knowing he'd gotten her off again clear to see. Then his eyes drifted shut, and he let himself go, fucking her harder and faster, the muscles in his neck standing out, his body taut, sweat beading on his chest and forehead. She saw his jaw clench, breath hissing from between his teeth, his back arching, his body shuddering as orgasm carried him away.

He dragged her with him deeper into the bed and settled onto his back, pillowing her head on his chest, his breathing gradually slowing, his fingers trailing up and down her spine. His tenderness surprised her. But then he'd already been so much more than she'd expected—more skilled, more thrilling, more intense. The last time she'd met a man who'd blown her away like this was… never.

She reached for his free hand, laced her fingers through his, sorry the night was over. Any minute now, he'd get up, get dressed, thank her for the good time, and head back to his own room. That's how it worked, how she preferred it.

Sex with no obligations.

"I'm not done with you," he said in a deep, sleepy voice, repeating what she'd said to him maybe an hour ago.

She tried not to notice her own sense of relief. "I sure as hell hope not."

And before she realized it, they were both asleep.

K *nock knock knock.*

"Room service."

Javier was awake and on his feet, taking in the situation at a glance. Shoes and clothes scattered across the floor. The bed covers a tangled mess. Laura still half-asleep and confused. Both of them naked.

The knock came again.

He grabbed for his clothes as he moved toward the bathroom. "You'd best put something on, *bella*. You've got company."

She muttered something under her breath in Swedish, hopping out of bed, her sexy ass catching his gaze as she ran to the closet and pulled out a blue silk bathrobe, slipping her arms into the sleeves and tying the belt around her waist. "Breakfast. I have a standing order for seven a.m. Damn!"

The strangeness of the situation made him grin, though he knew it shouldn't. If he were discovered here…

"I'll be in the bathroom." He made sure he had everything—shoes, socks, jeans, T-shirt, wallet—then glanced around the room for any sign that might give him away.

Knock knock knock knock.

"Miss Nilsson?" It was a woman's voice.

She spoke with an accent. Filipino?

"Just a moment, please!" Laura looked over at him, a hint of a smile on her panicked face, her fingers combing through the tangles in her hair. "I'm never undressed when they arrive."

And then he saw it.

He pointed with a jerk of his head. "The condom wrapper."

Laura glanced around, saw it lying on the floor near the wall not far inside the doorway, and picked it up. Looking confused about what to do with it, she opened the drawer of her bedside table and dropped it inside, glancing over at him as she hurried toward the door. "Go! Hide!"

But he had already ducked into the darkness of the bathroom. The tile floor cold against his feet, he listened as Laura opened the door and a hotel employee entered.

From covert ops in Afghanistan to an illicit hookup in Dubai.

What would JG and the guys think if they could see you now, cabrón?

They'd probably laugh their asses off.

"I'm sorry, Nadira. I worked late last night and overslept." Laura's voice sounded calm and cool, giving nothing away. "Please set the tray down on the table."

"Is there anything else I can get for you while I'm here, miss? Fresh towels for your morning bath?"

"No, thank you. As long as I have good strong coffee, I'll be fine."

"If you will sign for the meal, miss."

Silence.

"Thank you, Nadira."

"Thank you, miss. Have a good day."

A moment later, the door closed.

"The coast is clear," Laura called in a hushed voice.

He slipped into his jeans, zipped them, then stepped out of the bathroom, the scent of coffee luring him.

There on a large oval tray sat a plate with scrambled eggs, toast, and half a grapefruit. There was one cup, one set of silverware, one pot of coffee.

He picked up a piece of toast, took a bite. "This looks good, but what are you going to eat?"

CHAPTER FOUR

Javier prepared to return to his own room. Laura needed to get ready for a business meeting with her security team at nine and another with her bosses at the network at ten.

"What's your room number? I'll give you a buzz when I'm done."

"You do that." He gave her his room number, leaned down, and kissed her, some part of him reluctant to go.

He hit the gym, running a quick four miles on the treadmill and then doing his upper-body workout with free weights. His body felt great—strong, relaxed, in the zone.

That's because you got laid last night, chacho.

Hell, yeah, he had.

Vitamin P—it does a body good.

That's what Murphy, Delta Platoon's sniper, always said.

When he finished with his third set, Javier returned to his room and took a long, cool shower, rinsing away the sweat. He could still smell Laura on his skin, her musky scent making him half-hard. He dried off, dressed, ordered breakfast from room service, then sat down to check his email. By the time he'd finished, it was almost eleven, and he was beginning to feel restless, cooped up.

Chill out, brother. She'll call.

And if she didn't?

If she didn't, that was fine. They'd had a great time last night. Sure, he'd love to spend tonight in her bed. He was a straight, red-blooded male after all, and Laura was a whole lot more than he'd bargained for in the best possible way. But if she wasn't up for another round, he'd find some other way to pass the time.

It was almost noon when his phone finally rang.

"Meet me out front." It was Laura, her voice hushed. "We'll catch a cab to a place where we can be seen together. And Javier?"

He shoved his wallet in his back jeans pocket, grabbed his cell phone and his room key card. "Yeah?"

"Hurry! It's hot out here."

He found her standing in the shade outside the main doors, and damned if she didn't look cute. She was dressed in a hot pink V-neck T-shirt, a pair of designer jeans, and heels, a leather handbag on her shoulder, her long hair hanging down her back in pale blond waves. Somehow she managed to make even denim look classy.

She smiled at him from behind a pair of sunglasses, those dimples appearing in her cheeks. "Let's go."

He was struck by how young she looked, more like a college girl and less like an ass-kicking journalist. Then again, he had no idea how old she truly was. Watching her on TV, seeing her dressed in tailored pantsuits, he'd assumed she was in her thirties, but now he was almost afraid to guess.

A cab pulled up to the curb, and they climbed inside. She spoke in what sounded like Arabic to the driver, who grinned and shot out into traffic, his radio playing Top 40 hits from the '80s.

Javier resisted the urge to reach for her, to touch her. "Do I get to know where we're going, or is that a surprise?"

She smiled again. "You'll see."

They spent the next couple of hours at the Dubai Aquarium with its underwater tunnel. As amazing as the aquarium and underwater zoo were, Javier had spent his fair share of time diving, so the experience didn't give him the thrill that it seemed to give Laura, who smiled and laughed as a shark swam back and forth above their heads. Still, he wasn't about to complain. He had fun watching her have fun.

They grabbed a late lunch at a restaurant with a fancy Arabic name that served what Laura promised was the best Lebanese food in Dubai City, then went to a theater to catch *Iron Man*, sharing popcorn but unable even to hold hands. Still, Javier was aware of her beside him, a sensual tension stretching between them that fed his sexual need for her, his mind less on the film and more on what he wanted to do to her sweet body later.

Were hard-ons in the movie theater illegal, too?

If so, Javier would be facing twenty to life for sure.

By the time the film was over, the sun was about to set. They stopped for dinner at a café that was near a large artificial lake, Burj Khalifa rising into the sky across the water like some kind of vertical mirage, only parts of its highest reaches still unfinished. They talked about the film, which they'd both enjoyed.

"I just wish superheroes truly existed," Laura said, finishing her salad. "Terrible things happen in this world, and there doesn't seem to be anyone to stop them."

Some of us try, bella.

He thought the words, but he didn't say them. "Did you decide to come here yourself, or were you assigned to cover the war?"

"I had to fight like hell to get this assignment. They wanted to give it to a man because some people worried that audiences wouldn't take war coverage seriously if it were delivered by a woman. They also thought I was too young."

Javier saw his chance. "How old are you?"

"I'll tell you, but only if you do the same."

"Deal."

"I'm twenty-eight."

Twenty-eight.

Well, that wasn't bad. He was only six years older than she was, not enough to land him in the dirty-old-man category. "I'm thirty-four."

A smile lit up her beautiful face. "At last I know something about you."

He leaned forward. "All you need to know about me, *bella*, is that I'm the man who's going to make you scream."

She leaned in until her face was a mere inch from his, a teasing look in her eyes, her calf caressing his lower leg. "Promises, promises."

Then a murmur went up from the crowd.

Laura's face lit up. "*This* is what I wanted us to see. I saw photos of it last week in the *Khaleej Times*."

Javier looked over his shoulder and watched as the fountains in the lake came alive to the strains of what sounded like "Time to Say Goodbye," dancing jets of water lit from below by colored lights to form swaying circles, serpentine lines, and graceful whirling columns. He'd never seen anything like it.

"'*Con te partirò.*' Andrea Bocelli." Laura began to sing along softly in what sounded like Italian. Was there any language she didn't speak? "Oh, it's beautiful!"

"Yeah." But Javier's gaze was on Laura.

They took separate cabs back to the hotel, not wanting the staff there to see them together. By the time Laura got back to her room, she couldn't wait to get her hands on Javier. Not being able to touch him all day had been strangely titillating, his body like forbidden territory, all that man and muscle beyond her reach.

But not for much longer.

She ordered a bowl of fruit, a cheese tray, and champagne, knowing they'd both be hungry later.

"I have to work late tonight," she told the young woman who delivered it, adding a large tip to the bill and signing.

Did the girl suspect anything? It *was* a lot of food for one person. And who drank champagne alone?

But if she had any suspicions, the girl didn't let them show, thanking Laura and disappearing down the hall with her cart.

Laura took a quick shower, brushed her teeth, and smoothed cream onto her skin, her blood already running hot with memories of last night. How Javier had ripped her panties off, lifted her up, and fucked her against the wall. How he'd carried her to the bed and made her come with his mouth. How he'd driven into her, hard and deep, making her come again. He'd been forceful, strong, matching her libido at every turn, and she wanted more. But what could she do to raise the stakes tonight?

She slipped into the white silk mini-chemise she'd picked up at the Dubai Mall a few days ago, then retouched her makeup.

Her phone buzzed.

It was Javier. "On my way up. Coast clear?"

"Yes."

She turned down the lights in her room, opened the champagne, and poured a glass for them to share from the single flute the kitchen had provided. Then she stepped into the shadows and waited.

It didn't take long.

She heard his key card slide into the lock, heard the door buzz open.

He entered, put out the Do Not Disturb sign, and locked the door behind him. Then he turned toward her. "I've wanted you all damned day. I…"

She stepped out to where he could see her, his words trailing off as he looked her over, her pulse skipping at the naked hunger she saw in his eyes.

She handed him the champagne.

He took a sip, set the glass aside, and reached for her, drawing her against him, his lips coming down hard on hers. His tongue carried the taste of champagne into her mouth, his body hard and strong against hers, the urgency of his sexual need fueling hers.

Oh, God.

She'd been waiting all day for this, waiting to touch him, to kiss him, to feel his perfect male body pressed against her. And she realized that someone watching them might mistake them for lovers who'd been separated for months, rather than casual sex partners who'd only met last night.

She felt one of his hands close over her left breast, felt his thumb graze her nipple, scattering sparks deep inside her belly, making her wet. She was aching for him, already feeling the need to have him inside her. But this wasn't what she'd planned.

She drew back, her heart thrumming. She didn't want to lose herself in him. Not yet. "Take off your clothes."

He did as she asked, dropping his shirt on the floor, kicking off his shoes, shucking his jeans. She took in the sight of him, his firm muscles, his smooth skin, his delicious cock growing hard and thick while she watched.

Her gaze locked with his as she knelt before him and wrapped her hand around his erection. She teased the engorged head with her tongue, tasting along its thick rim, flicking the sensitive spot on the underside, lapping at the pre-cum that oozed from the slit at its tip, his male scent filling her head.

Breath left his lungs in a slow exhale, his fingers sliding into her hair.

She drew his foreskin up over the head, sucked on it, then teased the head through that thin layer of tender skin, gratified by the way his brow furrowed and his jaw went tight, his fingers delving deeper into her hair. Then she went to work, drawing the foreskin back and moving her hand and mouth in tandem up and down the length of his cock, catching the head with her tongue on each pass, reaching with her other hand to cup and fondle his balls.

He moaned and his head fell back, their eye contact broken.

God, it turned her on to turn him on.

His hips began to move, his abdominal muscles flexing, his grip on her hair getting tighter, and she felt a trickle of moisture between her thighs.

Then he stopped her. "You like that, don't you, *bella*?"

"Yeah, I do." She licked him, pleased by the way a flick of her tongue could make his cock jerk. "I like being in control, seeing the effect I have on you."

"Is that so?" His lips curved into a lethal smile.

In a heartbeat, she found herself lifted off her feet and pinned face down on the bed, her body lying across his lap. One of his big hands held her right arm behind her back, while the other hand pushed up her chemise to fondle her bare bottom.

"God, I love your ass."

She had no idea where he was going with this. "I don't do anal."

"Easy, *bella*. Neither do I."

The spanking took her by complete surprise.

She gasped, her ass stinging where he'd slapped her, the sting turning to tingles that raised goose bumps across her buttocks. She struggled to turn over, but couldn't budge, his strength holding her still. "What the hell are you—?"

"How does it feel when you're not in control?"

She bit back profanity, a part of her really pissed off. But there was another part of her, some strange, unfamiliar part, that had just been awakened and seemed to *enjoy* this—especially when he followed that little slap with a caress.

"Answer me. How does it feel when you're not in control?" He slapped her ass again, harder this time, his warm palm soothing the sting.

She bit back a moan, pain melting into heat. "It makes me *angry*."

"Yeah?" He slapped her again and again, then caressed her, one of his fingers angling between her buttocks, finding her vagina, testing her. "You're wet, *bella*. You like this. Admit it."

"Giving you head is what made me wet, not *this*." She squirmed, her thighs instinctively parting to give him access.

"You're lying." He spanked her again—hard.

She moaned, her vaginal muscles clenching around emptiness as pain once more transformed into pleasure, her skin seeming to shiver. "Oh, yes!"

Laura surrendered as Javier got down to work, taking time between sharp, little spankings to play between her thighs, stroking her wet entrance, parting her lips, teasing her aching clit.

He leaned down, nipped her shoulder. "Oh, yeah, you like this. Feel how swollen your clit is."

The skin of her buttocks was hypersensitive now, tingling, burning, the scorching sensation settling between her thighs as he fingered her deeply. And she realized he'd released her arm. He wasn't holding her down now. Nothing was forcing her to lie here—apart from her own relentless hunger.

She lifted her ass, parted her thighs, her hands fisting the bed sheets, her breath coming in pants and whimpers as he gave her the most incredible finger-fuck she'd ever had, the pleasure punctuated by sharp, stinging slaps.

She came with a cry, the barrage of sensations sending her over the top, the bliss of it singing through her, his fingers driving her home.

The tremors of her orgasm hadn't yet faded when he dragged her to the center of the bed, grabbed her hips, and drew her onto all fours, lifting her ass upward, nudging her thighs apart with his own. Desire flared to life again, fueled by the excitement of his domination.

"Ass up, thighs apart!" He gave her another quick spanking, the head of his cock nudging against her pussy.

"*Yes!*" Oh, she wanted him inside her *now*.

He entered her with a single deep thrust, filling and stretching her, his possession of her absolute. He gave her a few slow strokes, and then he was fucking her deep and hard. His hand fisted in her hair and pulled, forcing her head back, this slight pain arousing her even more, her body tingling from her scalp to the tender skin of her ass as he drove himself into her.

She had never been dominated like this by a man before, would never have imagined she would enjoy it. But there was something about Javier, something that made her want to submit to him, to surrender, to let him take control. He wasn't even touching her clit and yet she was on the edge, about to come again.

"Oh, Javi! Yes!" Pleasure drew tight in her belly—then exploded.

She couldn't help but cry out, the intensity off the scale as he pounded himself into her, finishing with a deep groan.

Spent, he bent over her, pressing kisses against the skin of her back, whispering to her in breathless Spanish. "*Mi dulce, preciosa belleza.*"

Then he stretched out beside her, drew her into his arms, and held her.

And through a post-orgasmic haze, Laura found herself wondering whether she'd ever felt this close to a man before.

CHAPTER FIVE

"The winters are long and dark in Stockholm—cold, rainy."
Content and sleepy, Javier sat against the back of the tub, holding Laura against his chest, one hand idly caressing a soft breast while she told him about her life growing up in Sweden, the fruit and cheese long since devoured, the champagne gone. He kissed her hair, a strange tenderness for her stirring inside him.

He'd never taken things that far before—spanking a woman, pulling her hair. Something about Laura provoked him, her sexual assertiveness goading him, her desire for control a challenge he hadn't been able to resist.

So you've got a streak of Boricua *machismo after all,* cabrón.

He'd found himself wanting to possess her completely. And, God, it had turned him on—watching her creamy ass turn pink, seeing goose bumps dance across her skin, feeling her grow wetter and hornier by the second.

"We had a sauna in our backyard that my grandfather built." Her fingers brushed lazy circles on his thigh. "When it was really cold, we would undress and sit together in the steam to keep warm and stay healthy. My mother—"

"You didn't sit in there naked." Obviously he needed to pay better attention, because he couldn't have understood her correctly.

She laughed. "Who wears clothes into a sauna?"

"But you must have wrapped yourselves in towels or something."

"We put the towels on the benches. The wood gets very hot."

"So you sat in a sauna with your entire family, and you all saw each other naked." Javier couldn't imagine his family doing that. He shut his mind against the idea before a horrifying image of his naked *abuelos* could form in his head.

"It's really no big deal. Everyone has a body, you know."

"That doesn't mean I want to *see* them."

His mother? His grandmother? His aunties?

¡Pal carajo! Oh, hell, no!

But Laura was laughing. "I guess we have a different attitude toward nudity in Scandinavia."

"That's the truth."

It helped explain why she seemed so at ease with her naked body. She was one of the few women he'd been with who hadn't cut herself down in some way or tried to get reassurance from him that her butt wasn't fat or her breasts weren't too small or too big or too saggy. He could get used to that. Confidence was sexy.

He nuzzled her ear, ran a thumb over her nipple, watched it pucker. "Did you go topless on the beach?"

"Of course."

The idea of a teenage Laura prancing around in public wearing nothing but bikini bottoms sent a surge of heat to his groin.

You're scum, Corbray.

Incredibly, he began to get hard again, his erection pressing against her hip. He'd thought he was finished for the night, but being near her like this had apparently given his cock other ideas. She was a living, breathing aphrodisiac.

He pressed kisses along her throat, both hands fondling her breasts now, teasing their sensitive tips, the part of him that had wanted to possess her earlier now longing to show her gentleness.

Her head lolled to the side, her eyes drifting shut as he kissed and nibbled his way along her pulse. "Javi, what have you done to me? These past two days…"

He bit her earlobe. "Just enjoy the ride."

He nudged his legs between hers, bent his knees and spread them, forcing her legs apart. Reaching with one hand to cup her, his fingers caught and stretched her inner lips and her clit while his fingertips circled the still-slick entrance to her vagina. Soon, her breathing was ragged, each exhale a sexy little moan, her head rolling slowly from side to side on his chest, her nails digging into his thighs.

He angled his hips to enter her from behind, her pussy closing around him, wet and hot, as he thrust inside her. He fucked her slow and easy, determined to give them both all the sexual pleasure they could take, this position allowing him to pamper her, to touch and tease her everywhere— those sweet rosy nipples, the sensitive skin of her inner thighs, her swollen clit.

He'd spent years training his body, learning to use it as a weapon, teaching it to respond to his will. Now he used that training to slow himself down, willing his muscles to relax, holding his own climax at bay. He drew slow breaths, his head falling back.

And then he saw.

The ceiling above the tub was a mirror.

"Laura, look up."

She did as he asked, her breath catching when she saw the mirror reflecting the two of them in flawless detail—their faces, the crystalline surface of the water, the joining of their bodies. "Oh! I can see *everything*."

He reached down, caught her thighs, and drew her knees back. "Now watch while I make you come."

He thrust into her until he was completely buried, nothing visible but his balls, the rest of him deep inside her, then withdrew again, his dark cock stretching her rosy entrance, her labia parted, her clit swollen and pink.

"That's… so… *sexy*, so… *erotic*." Her words unraveled on a moan.

Hell, yeah, it was.

Sexy. Erotic. So fucking hot.

Heart slamming in his chest, he thrust inside her again, the rhythm building until he was ramming himself into her fast and hard, both of them watching, the carnal sight pushing Javier close to the edge. And when at last Laura came, Javier came with her, pleasure flooding them both.

L aura opened the door to her room and set the tray holding the dirty dishes from last night down in the hallway, pretending not to notice the maid who stood outside the room across from hers organizing bed linens on a cleaning cart. She shut the door and locked it, whispering to Javier. "She's still out there."

"I'm hungry, man. Can't she go clean someplace else?" He peeked out the security peephole, muttered profanity in Spanish.

Laura hated having to sneak around like this. "We could split an omelet or something."

"Wait." He held up a finger. "She's turning toward the vacuum. Okay, this is it, *bella*. I'll meet you out front in twenty."

He kissed her on the cheek, opened the door, and disappeared down the hallway just as the maid turned her back toward Laura's room and started the vacuum, its loud whir drowning out any noise he might have made. Laura kept the door open a crack to watch, giving a sigh of relief as he disappeared around the corner, heading for the stairs.

Quietly, she shut and locked the door, then hurried to take a shower, feeling both a little sore and brilliantly alive. Last night had been the most amazing night of sex she could remember. She wanted to believe it was because she'd pushed her boundaries and tried something new, but the truth had much more to do with how she'd felt about being with Javier, as if there were no barriers between them.

That's the difference between good sex and fan-freaking-tastic sex, Nilsson.

She slipped into a vintage dress of filmy rose-colored georgette, cinched it with a metallic gold belt, and put on gold sandals, grabbing a lightweight navy blazer to cover her shoulders in public and ward off air conditioning chill. A few swipes of mascara and some lip gloss, and she was ready.

Javier was waiting for her when she stepped out, the heat reminding her that it was almost midday. Wearing jeans, black boots, and a plain gray and white ringer T-shirt that seemed to emphasize his biceps, he pretended not to know her, but hailed a cab.

"Are you going to the Mall of the Emirates?" she asked as he climbed into the back seat. "Can we share the fare?"

They ate brunch together, then strolled through the mall, Laura amused by Javier's reaction to the merchandise.

"More than a hundred grand for a diamond-studded cell phone. You could buy a house with that."

Laura laughed. "Not here you couldn't."

"Right."

She bought a small bottle of perfume from her favorite parfumier, while he bought a single postcard, one that showed the highlights of the city—Sheikh Zayed Road, the Atlantis Hotel, Jumeirah Beach, and Burj Al Arab.

"I thought you weren't impressed by the sights here."

"This is for my *abuelita*," he explained. "She likes to see where I've been. I'll be home before she gets it, but she'll love it anyway."

"Aw, that's sweet."

He grinned. "Hey, I'm all heart."

And then it hit her in a way it hadn't before.

In a little more than twelve hours, Javier would be leaving Dubai City, and that would be the end. She wouldn't see him again.

They ended up at an expat beach party, more because it allowed them to let down their guard and be themselves than because they actually wanted to be there. It looked like a hundred other beach parties Javier had been to, alcohol flowing freely, loud music, men and women laughing, dancing, holding hands. But he didn't need to look at the glittering skyline to know he wasn't in San Diego. There was a kind of frenetic energy in the crowd, as if everyone were trying hard to convince themselves they were having the time of their lives, their conversation revolving as often as not around wealth—who was rich, who'd just made bank, who they thought was going to hit it big next.

Javier bought a couple of drinks, guiding Laura away from the crowd, only too aware of the way people watched her, obviously recognizing her. They ended up walking the length of the beach, Javier answering her questions about summers spent as a child in Puerto Rico. It felt good just to walk beside her, their fingers intertwined, the sound of the surf around them. And not for the first time he found himself wishing tonight weren't their last night together. He hadn't gotten enough of her—not by a long shot.

"My brothers, sisters, cousins, and I ran wild from the time the sun came up, playing baseball, swimming in the surf, digging in the sand."

"I bet you got into a lot of trouble." Her lips curved in a little smile.

"Hell, yeah, I did." There was more truth to that than she would ever know. But that was the advantage of a relationship like this. She would only ever see him at his best. "When it got dark, someone's mother would call us in for supper. Mamá Andreína would feed us, throw us in the tub, and put us to bed."

"That sounds like a wonderful way to grow up."

"It was." He hadn't spoken with many people about his childhood. His brother Yadiel's death made that too painful. But talking to Laura was as easy and natural as breathing. "My brothers and I fell asleep every night to the singing of *coquís*."

"What's a … *coquí*?"

"You don't know about *coquís*?" He found himself chuckling. "They're frogs. They live in the rainforest and the parks, and they sing all night."

He did his best to imitate their high-pitched call, more of a whistle really.

She gave him a skeptical look, one graceful blond brow arched. "That sounds more like a bird than a frog. Frogs say 'ribbit.'"

"Not in Puerto Rico, *bella*." He did his *coquí* imitation again. "They *do* sound more like birds—you're right about that. And they are tiny—but very loud."

They reached the beach marker that indicated the end of the hotel's property and stopped, turning to look out at the dark water. The breeze caught her hair, the hem of her dress. God, she was beautiful.

"Where will you be this time tomorrow?" she asked, her hand warm in his.

He did a little math. "I'll be about to land at JFK. How about you?"

"They haven't sorted out my visa problems, so it looks like I'll be staying here for a few more days." There was a tone of resignation to her voice.

"Where are you headed next?"

She looked up at him, an apology written on her face. "I can't talk about it. I *wish* I could. I trust you, but my security contract—"

"No worries. I understand." He leaned down and kissed her. "Dance with me?"

In the distance he could hear "Time to Say Goodbye" playing as the Dubai Fountain put on a show for another nighttime crowd.

She rested her hand in his, her other arm going around his shoulder as she slipped into his arms. "I've had such a great time with you."

"Same here." He smiled. "It's not over yet, *bella*."

They danced slow circles in the sand, Javier singing the words to the Spanish version of the song, the melancholy music putting a strange ache in his chest, an ache he saw reflected in her eyes. Was she feeling what he was feeling?

And what exactly *was* he feeling? He wasn't sure. He only knew that he wasn't ready for this to end—and that he wanted to kiss her.

He leaned down and took her lips with his. This wasn't the mild peck on the cheek a married man might be able to give his wife in public in Dubai. It was a full-on, open-mouthed kiss that involved tongue, lips, teeth. And it made him want more.

You're playing with fire, cabrón.

They were far from the anonymity of the crowd now, standing where they could be seen, a man and woman alone together, kissing and holding each other tight.

He drew back. "What do you say we ditch this scene and make the most of tonight back in your hotel room?"

She nodded. "I'd like that."

In the distance, they could hear the crowd at the fountain applauding.

CHAPTER SIX

Laura walked through the hotel's doors and went straight up to her room, Javier not far behind. Their slow dance on the beach and that long, scorching kiss had left her ravenous for him, her need accentuated by knowing that he was leaving in the morning.

Tomorrow night, she would sleep alone.

That's just how it was, of course. She'd been lucky in this big, crazy world to come across a man like him, a man she could enjoy herself with so completely, a man who not only made her body sing, but also respected her boundaries and her career.

He arrived at her door moments after she did, the intensity and urgency she saw in his eyes a match for what she felt.

She reached for him, took his hand, and led him to the shower, eager to rinse away the day's heat and sand. They wasted no time, undressing one another with impatient tugs, stepping together into the warm spray.

Javier grabbed the soap first. He turned her away from him and drew her back against him, lathering his hands, then rubbing them over her body, taking extra time with her breasts. "Does that feel good, *bella*?"

The feel of his soap-slick hands on her wet skin unleashed a flood of heat between her thighs. "*Yeah.*"

"*Bien.*" He plucked her nipples, drew them to hard peaks, the sensation almost unbearably arousing. "How about now?"

"Even ... *better.*" She felt her legs go weak and reached out to press one hand against the tile wall to steady herself, her fingers slowly sliding down the slick surface.

He wrapped a strong arm around her waist, the other hand forsaking her breasts to rub soap over her belly, her hips, her bottom. "You have the *sexiest* ass."

He stepped aside, let the water rinse the lather away. Then he bent her forward and forced her feet apart. "Spread your legs."

She did as he asked, expecting to feel a sharp sting any second, the memory of last night's sexy spankings making her bite her lower lip with anticipation.

Instead of spanking her, he knelt behind her, spread her with his hands, and nipped her ass—one fierce little bite. "I want your scent on me, all over my skin, down my throat. I want to take it home with me."

In the next instant he was tasting her, his tongue sliding a serpentine path from her clit to the opening of her vagina. "Mmm."

"*Javi!*" If her fingers could have dug into the tiles, they would have. She clawed at the wet wall, locked her knees, afraid her legs might give out.

He lapped at her, teased her entrance, moving his head back and forth as if he were trying to bury his face in her, the vigorous motion carrying his tongue back and forth across her clit.

She'd always loved both getting and giving head, but this was something else, the sensation so raw that she was afraid she'd come too fast to savor it. And she *wanted* to savor it. She willed her vagina not to tighten, tried to relax and just let the erotic thrill of being devoured by him carry her along, her cheek now pressed against the tile, her breath coming in ragged pants.

But then he thrust his tongue inside her—and she shattered.

She cried out, her orgasm so intense that she reached down between her thighs to cup herself as if to hold herself together, his tongue fucking her, forcing its way past her clenching muscles to stroke her until at last her climax had passed. She sagged against the cold wall, breathing hard.

But he wasn't finished.

He drew her upright and turned her in his arms, his mouth coming down on hers, her own musky taste exploding across her tongue. He caught her left leg with his hand and wrapped it around his waist, his breath leaving his lungs in a rush as he slid inside her. "You are so tight, so sweet."

She clung to him, her senses filled with him as he picked up the rhythm, his powerful thrusts carrying them both over the edge.

L aura turned off the water, resting her head against the hard wall of Javier's chest, his arms encircling her, his heart thudding as hard as hers. The bathroom air was heavy with the scent of sex, his salt and her musk mingling in the steam. She might have stayed like that forever had the hotel phone on her night stand not begun to ring.

"*Helvete!*" She pushed out of the shower stall, grabbing a towel and wrapping it around herself as she ran to answer. She reached it on the fourth ring. "Laura Nilsson."

"Miss Nilsson," a man's voice said, "I am sorry to disturb you, but we have received a complaint about noise coming from your room. Your neighbor said it sounded as if you were screaming or fighting with someone."

Laura's pulse skipped, her mind racing.

Think fast, Nilsson, or get ready for a few years in prison.

She let a quaver come into her voice. "I-I'm very sorry. I received some very upsetting news from home tonight. I was … crying. I didn't realize I was disturbing anyone."

She looked up to see Javier listening, a towel wrapped around his narrow hips, beads of water on his bare chest. He moved quickly and silently to the door, looked out the security peephole, then glanced over at her and shook his head.

No one was listening in the hallway.

"I am very sorry to hear that, Miss Nilsson. Is there any way we at the Radisson may be of help to you?"

"I'm afraid not. There's nothing to do now but pray for my grandmother." Laura hated to lie, but she was pretty sure she'd hate prison more.

"I will keep her in my prayers, Miss Nilsson. So sorry to have troubled you."

"I'm the one who is sorry. I let myself get carried away." Yes, she had, but with sexual bliss, not with grief or worry. "I'll make certain not to disturb anyone further."

The man wished her a good-night and hung up.

Laura did the same, then turned and glared at Javier, fighting not to laugh.

He shrugged, an innocent look on his face that had no right to be there. "What? *You* were the one who screamed."

She tried not to smile. "You *made* me do it."

A grin spread on those magical lips of his. "I told you I would."

Javier finished addressing the postcard he planned to mail to Mamá Andreína and set it together with the pen he'd borrowed on Laura's nightstand. "How long has it been since you've been home—and where *is* home, exactly?"

They lounged naked on the bed facing each other, sharing a bowl of Medjool dates, Javier trying to stay aware of the time.

As much as he wanted to ignore the clock, he knew he had to leave her soon. It was already nearing midnight, and he had an early flight. He still needed to pack his duffel, confirm his reservation, print out his boarding pass, get some sleep.

Then again, who needed sleep? He could sleep on the plane.

"I have a flat in Manhattan, but I haven't been there for almost six months." She nibbled a date, daintily prying the pit out with her fingers. "I spent my last vacation with my mother and grandmother in Stockholm. I've been leasing the place to another reporter."

A flat in Manhattan.

Not bad for a twenty-eight-year-old single woman.

"It must get lonely."

She gave a little shrug. "Sometimes, but someone has to do this job. It's important that people back home know what's going on. Maybe it sounds egotistical, but I'm a good journalist. I want to do my part."

"It doesn't sound egotistical. It's the truth. You *are* good."

"Besides, Chris, my cameraman, and I are good friends. He spends more time with me than he does his wife. And Nico, Cody, and Tim—that's my security team—they're a lot of fun when they're not being grumpy and serious."

"You and a bunch of guys, huh?" Javier tried to ignore a stab of possessiveness.

As long as they keep her safe, why do you care, pendejo?

Because he did. That's why.

A slow smile spread across her face. She set the bowl of dates aside and pushed him onto his back, pinning his wrists above his head and leaning over him, her hair spilling around their faces. "Why, Javier Corbray, are you jealous?"

"Why should I be?" She was playing at control again, and he let her have her way, enjoying the sight of her incredible breasts so close to his mouth. "They're not here with you. *I* am."

"That's right." She leaned down, brushed a kiss over his lips, her voice sexy-soft. "I've never kissed any of them."

"That's good."

She sat back, raked her nails none too gently down his chest. "I sure as hell never let any of them spank me."

"Oh, I have no doubt about that."

She reached back, her arm disappearing behind her, one hand closing around his half-hard cock. "I've never seen them naked or given them head."

Heat filled his groin as she stroked him to readiness.

"And I've never had any of them inside me." She raised herself up, lowering herself onto him, guiding his cock into her pussy, taking all of him.

Paradise.

He grasped her hips to steady her as she settled herself, leaving it to her to set the pace. "God, I love your body."

She smiled, her expression changing to one of sensual pleasure as she rode him, her pace nice and easy, her palms resting on his chest for balance, her clit grinding against his pubic bone. "Give a girl a hand?"

But he was already on it, cupping her breasts, flicking her nipples with his thumbs, plucking them, rolling them between his fingers, gratified by her shuddering exhale—and the way she grew even wetter.

He wanted more. "Feed me."

He slid his hands behind her, guiding her down, his mouth capturing her puckered nipples, suckling them.

She moaned, a soft, breathy sound, resting her hands against the headboard, her hips moving faster.

It was enough to drive Javier crazy, but not enough to make him come. Still, he could tell it was perfect for her, and that was good enough—for now.

Using one hand to guide her breasts, he slid the other between their bodies and pressed the pad of his thumb just above her clit, moving it in a circular motion, adding pressure.

"Yes!" She moaned out his name, riding him hard now.

He felt her vagina tighten around him, felt her body tense, and just had time to put a hand over her mouth to silence her cry before she came.

She kept up her rhythm until the tremors inside her had passed, then sagged against him, boneless and breathless.

Still hard and buried inside her, he gave her a moment to catch her breath, and then retook control, flipping her onto her back and pinning her arms over her head as she'd done to him. But, unlike her, he had the physical strength to make it real.

"It's my turn."

She struggled just enough to test him, her pupils dilating when she realized she truly was pinned down, hunger on her face. "Fuck me."

He hammered into her with thrusts that shook the bed, her legs spread wide, her feet resting on his ass, her little moans like music to him. God, it felt good, being inside her like this, her sweet pussy gripping him, her amazing body his to savor. He wanted to stay just like this all night—hard, inside her, on the edge.

He looked down at her sweet face, and something strange happened.

He stopped moving and found himself reaching with one hand to cradle her cheek, sexual need melting into tenderness. He pressed his forehead to hers, their gazes locking. *"Laura."*

Her hands slid up his chest to caress his jaw. "Kiss me."

He did, moving inside her again, sliding in and out of her with slow strokes, aware of every breath she took, every sound she made, every emotion that stirred behind her blue eyes. *"Bella."*

And when they came, their breathy sighs mingling in a long, desperate kiss, Javier realized he'd never felt this connected to any other woman.

It was the sound of a closing door that woke him.

Javier opened his eyes, looked down to see Laura curled up against his chest. He stroked her hair and closed his eyes—then sat upright with a jolt. "¡*Puñeta*!"

Had he missed his flight?

"Fuck!" He glanced at the clock on her nightstand, saw that it was almost seven.

Laura sat up, the sheet falling away from her bare breasts, her hair tousled. "What's wrong?"

"I overslept." He hadn't meant to sleep at all, at least not in Laura's room. "I needed to be at the airport a half hour ago, and I still have to pack."

It wasn't like him to be forgetful or late.

He jumped out of bed and went in search of his clothes.

She was on her feet, hurrying through the suite, handing him his jeans, a sock, his boxer briefs. "A cab will get you there in about ten minutes. If you hurry, you can make it before seven-thirty. What time does your flight leave?"

"Eight-thirty." He dressed quickly.

"As long as you're there at least an hour early, you should be able to make your flight. After seven-thirty, they won't let you board."

He finished buttoning his shirt, glancing around to see if he'd left anything else, anything that might get her into trouble.

And then it hit him.

This was goodbye.

He reached for her, drew her naked body into his arms, and pressed a kiss to her cheek. "I had a great time, *bella*. You're an incredible woman."

The words sounded meaningless, far too casual for what he was feeling. He wanted to ask for her phone number and email, wanted to give her his, wanted to tell her that he'd love to see her again, that if she ever needed him, he would be there for her. But he had agreed that their weekend would be a weekend—nothing more.

Now the weekend was over.

No strings.

Why in the hell did you agree to that, cabrón?

She stood on tiptoe, kissed him, the sweet scent of sex still on her skin. "Thank you, Javi. You're the best time ever. Now go."

He looked down at her, some part of him rooted to the spot, wanting to make this moment different, but not knowing how to do that. "Stay safe."

She smiled. "You too—whatever it is you do."

He handed her the extra key card, then turned and walked out of her life like he'd promised her he would.

But by the time he reached the elevators, he'd made another promise—this one to himself. One day, he would track her down.

And next time, he wouldn't let her go so easily.

L aura sat on the edge of the bed, clutching her bathrobe around her and staring at the closed door, feeling strangely naked and alone. She'd known she would have to say goodbye to Javier today, she just hadn't expected it to be so abrupt. Nor had she expected it to leave her feeling so ... *desolate*.

She reached over, ran her hand over the sheets, the bed still warm from his body heat, his scent still on her skin. "Goodbye, Javi."

It was the pricking of tears in her eyes that got her to her feet.

"What's the matter with you, Nilsson?"

She wasn't usually this sentimental. Then again, she didn't usually hook up with men she didn't know and spend three days having sex with them—incredible, mind-blowing sex. Most of her lovers—really, there hadn't been all that many—had been men she'd dated before ending up in bed with them.

Javier had come out of nowhere. He'd given her more than she could have imagined. And now he was gone.

But wasn't this what she'd wanted, what they'd both wanted?

Yes, it was. They'd met, spent three amazing days together, had incredibly satisfying sex—okay, earth-shattering sex—and now it was time to move on. She should be happy that things had gone so well, not moping around her hotel room.

She walked to the window, drew back the curtains, willing herself to think about the day ahead. She needed to hit the gym, take a shower, and then give Nico a call to get an update on her visa situation. But first she wanted breakfast. She'd just reached for the phone to place an order with room service when she saw it.

Javier's postcard.

It sat on her nightstand, a message written in Spanish on the back along with his grandmother's name and an address in the Bronx. He had addressed it, but he hadn't put a stamp on it. She ran her fingers over the words he'd written and found herself smiling, her sense of desolation dissipating.

She was an investigative reporter. When she got back to the States, she would use his grandmother's address to track him down. She would find him.

One way or another, she would find Javier Corbray.

EPILOGUE

Two months later
San Diego, California

Javier stood on his deck with a few of his Team buddies grilling burgers and brats and shooting the shit. They'd just gotten word this morning that they'd be starting a month-long workup tomorrow and deploying in thirty days.

Nate West stepped outside, the look on his face telling Javier his phone call hadn't gone well. "Well, Rachel's pissed. She had her heart set on the Virgin Islands."

Javier gave his buddy a clap on the shoulder. "She needs to get used to this if she's marrying a military man."

"That's what I told her."

A Marine special operator whose team worked alongside Delta Platoon, West had become Javier's best friend. Though Javier would never tell his buddy this to his face, he knew West could do much better than Rachel. With his personality and good looks, he could snag any woman he wanted. He didn't need a spoiled brat for a wife.

A football flew through the air, narrowly missing Javier's head. "Get a grip on your balls, LeBlanc!"

"Sorry, senior chief!" LeBlanc called. "That was Murphy's fault."

"Yeah? Fuck you." Murphy apparently didn't agree. "If you'd caught the football, it wouldn't have nearly taken off senior's head."

"How can you be a crack sniper and throw like that?" LeBlanc fired back.

West cracked open a cold beer and handed it to Javier, a worried expression slowly replacing the amused grin his face. "Sometimes I wonder if she's ready for this. She knew I was a special operator before we got engaged."

If West was going to bring it up…

"Sounds like you should have a long talk about it, bro. If it's a problem now, what's it going to be like five years from now? I know it sounds harsh, but better a broken engagement than a divorce. Take my word for it." Javier took a drink, looked at the bottle. "Fat Tire?"

"A Colorado microbrew—my favorite."

The shit wasn't half-bad.

Javier flipped the burgers one last time. "They're done, boys."

If there was one thing the men of Delta Platoon did efficiently besides carrying out their Team missions, it was eating. The burgers and brats were gone in a matter of minutes. The men had just gathered on the deck, waiting for Javier to share what he knew about the workup when Javier saw the clock.

It was time for her broadcast.

He headed indoors, turned on his TV, and dropped onto the sofa, another beer in his hand. He looked over his shoulder, found the guys staring after him. "My favorite news program."

Ross grinned. "I think he's got a thing for the Baghdad Babe."

God, Javier hated that nickname!

He glared at Ross. "I like to keep up with world news and current events."

Snickers.

Okay, so they weren't buying that.

On the screen, Laura's anchor, Gary Chapin, was introducing the topic of the night's program, his helmet hair looking as stiff as it always did, an image of Laura in the upper right-hand corner of the screen.

Two months had gone by, and still he could remember her scent, her taste, the feel of her skin, the sound of her laughter, the gleam in her eyes. He hadn't given up on his plan to track down her contact info. Oh, no. He'd just gotten busy.

The guys crowded around him to watch.

And then she was on the screen, looking gorgeous, just like he remembered, her long, pale blond hair held back by a barrette.

"Yeah, she is fine!"

"Hot."

"Do you think she's a screamer?"

Their words made Javier's teeth grind.

¡Pendejos estupidos! Stupid assholes!

She looked into the camera, speaking with confidence, her voice soft but strong as steel as she explained how thousands of women died each year, burned to death by their husbands and in-laws so that their husbands could remarry, winning for themselves another woman's dowry. Though the dowry system was supposed to be illegal, the law was ignored. And in most cases, these horrible deaths were not investigated.

"That's fucking sick," Murphy said.

"Shhh!" Javier didn't want to listen to Murphy.

He wanted to hear Laura.

"In the past five years, Sabira Mukhari's organization has documented more than seven thousand five hundred cases of women being burned in 'stove accidents' within a two-hundred-mile radius around Islamabad and—"

A nearby door burst open, making Laura jump.

Rat-at-at-at-at-at!

AK fire.

On the TV screen, Laura screamed, dropped to the floor.

"What the fuck?" Javier was on his feet.

Men shouted in English and Arabic, her security team scrambling.

"Cover her! Cover her!"

A man in a black T-shirt threw himself over Laura, shielding her.

From somewhere, an M16 cut loose, and Javier thought one of the attackers was hit. But a man cried out, and the M16 went silent.

"Son of a fucking bitch!" Javier took two strides toward the TV screen, fists clenched, before he realized there was nothing—not a *goddamned* thing—he could do.

Her security detail was being massacred.

Rat-at-at-at-at-at!

More AK fire.

"Go, Laura!" A man cried out, groaned, blood spraying across the camera lens, women's screams coming from the background.

Out of view, Laura shouted to the other women in English, then in a language Javier didn't understand, terror in her voice. "Run! Get out! Go!"

But AK fire and screams told him that not all of them would make it.

Then two men dressed like Taliban or AQ operatives—olive green BDUs, head scarves—grabbed Laura off the floor, their bodies blocking the camera's view.

¡Madre de dios, no!

"Leave her the fuck alone!" Javier shouted. "Jesus Christ!"

He'd have given anything in the world to be there right now.

"No!" She kicked, screamed, seemed to fight with all her might as they carried her toward the door. "*Nooo!*"

And then she was gone.

The station shifted back to a stunned Gary Chapin.

Chills slid down Javier's spine, his gut churning. "*Bella!*"

Two days after her abduction, an Al-Qaeda splinter group headed by a fucker named Abu Nayef Al-Nassar took credit for abducting Laura—and claimed to have decapitated her.

The news struck Javier with the force of a grenade. He drifted through the day, feeling sick, doing his best to guide the men through the second day of their workup, trying to turn grief into anger.

"Shit like this is why we fight," he told them with a calm he did not feel.

It was only when he got home that he'd been able to take off his mask, grief tearing him apart, memories haunting him.

Laura. Bella.

She'd been so alive and vibrant, so intelligent, so sensual and beautiful. He remembered kissing and nipping her graceful neck, groaning against her throat—a throat that some son of a bitch had cut. Unable to bear that last thought, he stumbled out of his BDUs and stepped into a hot shower, rage erupting from inside him until he found himself beating on the tile wall with his fist. "No! No! No!"

For the second time in his life, Javier felt tears in his eyes.

"*María, madre de Dios, por favor, prométeme que Laura no sufrió.*"

Mary, mother of God, please promise me that Laura didn't suffer.

No answering voice came to reassure him.

He had no idea how long he stayed in the shower, how long he wept for her. He knew only that the water had turned cold. He stepped out, dried off, and looked at his own reflection in the mirror, making himself a promise.

One way or another, he would bring that motherfucker Al-Nassar down.

Want to know what happens next?

Order *Striking Distance* (I-Team Book 6) now, and read the rest of Javier and Laura's story. To read the prologue to *Striking Distance*, visit www.pamelaclare.com.

PRAISE FOR *STRIKING DISTANCE*

"This sixth I-Team installment sees Clare at her very best, combining scorching desire with a gripping, often painful, exploration of healing and redemption. The plot's mystery and suspense elements are exceptionally well researched and expertly plotted, but the real achievement lies in her beautifully crafted main couple. Her heroine's ordeal is unspeakably painful, but her strength never wavers. The chemistry with her steadfast hero never lacks for sizzle, but the emotional bond they share allows them to go beyond the physical to a profound, unforgettable love."

— **RT Book Reviews, 4.5 stars Top Pick for *Striking Distance***

"Packed with action and raw, sexual tension, Pamela Clare's Striking Distance *brings readers the edgy suspense, meaty subject matter, and intense emotions fans have come to expect from this talented author."*

—**Cindy Gerard, New York Times best-selling author.**

ALSO BY PAMELA CLARE

Historical Romance

Kenleigh-Blakewell Family Saga

Sweet Release (Book 1)

Carnal Gift (Book 2)

Ride the Fire (Book 3)

MacKinnon's Rangers series

Surrender (Book 1)

Untamed (Book 2)

Defiant (Book 3)

Upon A Winter's Night (Book 3.5)

Romantic Suspense

The I-Team Series

Extreme Exposure (Book 1)

Heaven Can't Wait: An I-Team novella (Book 1.5)

Hard Evidence (Book 2)

Unlawful Contact (Book 3)

Naked Edge (Book 4)

Breaking Point (Book 5)

Skin Deep: An I-Team After Hours novella (Book 5.5)

Striking Distance (Book 6)

ABOUT THE AUTHOR

Colorado author Pamela Clare began her writing career as a columnist and investigative reporter and eventually became the first woman editor-in-chief of two different newspapers. Along the way, she and her team won numerous state and national honors, including the National Journalism Award for Public Service. In 2011, Clare was awarded the Keeper of the Flame Lifetime Achievement Award. A single mother with two sons, she writes historical romance and contemporary romantic suspense at the foot of the beautiful Rocky Mountains. To learn more about her or her books, visit her website. You can also keep up with her on Goodreads, on Facebook, on the Rock*It Reads website, or by joining the private Facebook I-Team group. Search for @Pamela_Clare on Twitter to follow her there.

Printed in Great Britain
by Amazon.co.uk, Ltd.,
Marston Gate.